This Book Belongs
to: Miss. Sachi
Chamberlin

Milly and Molly

For my grandchildren
Thomas, Harry, Ella and Madeleine

Milly, Molly and Aunt Maude

Copyright © Milly Molly Books, 2002

Gill Pittar and Cris Morrell assert the moral right to
be recognized as the author and illustrator of this work.

Published by
Milly Molly Books
P O Box 539
Gisborne, New Zealand
email: books@millymolly.com

Printed by Rhythm Consolidated Berhad, Malaysia

ISBN: 1-86972-014-8

10   9   8   7   6   5   4   3   2   1

Milly, Molly
and
Aunt Maude

"We may look different
but we feel the same."

Aunt Maude had the best vegetable garden
in the world. Every vegetable you could
think of, grew in straight tidy rows.

One day, Milly and Molly found Aunt
Maude lying among her tomato plants.

"What a lovely place to die," she sighed.
"You're not going to die," said Doctor Smiley.
"You've broken your leg. In six weeks, you'll
be back on your feet again."

"Six weeks!" cried Aunt Maude. "I can't leave my vegetables for six weeks."

"We'll take care of your vegetables,"
said Milly. "And we'll get a pair of knitting
needles and some wool for you to make a
winter blanket," said Molly.

"What a good idea," said Doctor Smiley.
"I don't like knitting," snapped Aunt Maude.
"I would rather be out in my vegetable garden."

Aunt Maude started knitting slowly ... with
a lot of fuss.

At the end of the week, she was still knitting...
with less fuss.

By the end of the month, she was knitting madly... with no fuss at all.

"There you are," said Doctor Smiley. "Six weeks are up. Now you can go back to your vegetable garden."

"I'm not ready for the vegetable garden," snapped Aunt Maude.

"When will you be ready?" asked Milly.
"I don't know," snapped Aunt Maude.

"When will you stop knitting blankets?"
asked Molly.
"When I'm ready," snapped Aunt Maude.

Aunt Maude's pile of blankets grew bigger
and bigger. Milly and Molly wound all the
left-over wool into balls and they gardened...
and gardened.

When Aunt Maude disappeared behind her
pile of blankets, Milly whispered to Molly,
"I think we should call Doctor Smiley."

"What's the problem, Aunt Maude?"
asked Doctor Smiley kindly.

"There's no problem," snapped Aunt Maude.
"Well," said Doctor Smiley, "this time there's
nothing I can do."

Then it started to snow. Milly and Molly
battled to save the vegetable garden.

Doctor Smiley struggled to take care of
everyone with winter chills in his hospital.

"I have a problem of epidemic proportions,"
he told Aunt Maude. "I need more blankets."

By mid-morning, there wasn't a blanket left.

By mid-afternoon, Milly and Molly were
admitted to the hospital with exhaustion
and chills.

And by midnight, Aunt Maude had used the
leftover balls of wool to finish two more warm
blankets... one for Milly and one for Molly.

The next morning Aunt Maude was finally
ready. It stopped snowing and she went
back to her vegetable garden.

Milly, Molly and Aunt Maude

The Value implicitly expressed in this story is 'tenacity' - holding fast, stubborn.

Milly and Molly held fast to their kind offer to work in Aunt Maude's vegetable garden.
They did not give in to the snow.

"We may look different but we feel the same."

BOOKS

Other picture books in the Milly, Molly series include:

- Milly, Molly and Jimmy's Seeds   ISBN 1-86972-000-8
- Milly, Molly and Beefy   ISBN 1-86972-006-7
- Milly, Molly and Pet Day   ISBN 1-86972-004-0
- Milly, Molly and Oink   ISBN 1-86972-002-4
- Milly and Molly Go Camping   ISBN 1-86972-003-2
- Milly, Molly and Betelgeuse   ISBN 1-86972-005-9
- Milly, Molly and Taffy Bogle   ISBN 1-86972-001-6
- Milly, Molly and Alf   ISBN 1-86972-018-0
- Milly, Molly and Sock Heaven   ISBN 1-86972-015-6
- Milly, Molly and the Sunhat   ISBN 1-86972-016-4
- Milly, Molly and Special Friends   ISBN 1-86972-017-2
- Milly, Molly and Different Dads   ISBN 1-86972-019-9